CAROLYN BECK

THAT SQUEAK

Illustrated by

FRANÇOIS THISDALE

Fitzhenry & Whiteside

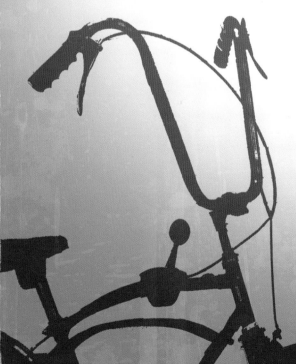

Published in Canada by Fitzhenry & Whiteside, 195 Allstate Parkway, Markham, Ontario L3R 4T8

Published in the United States by Fitzhenry & Whiteside, 311 Washington Street, Brighton, Massachusetts 02135

www.fitzhenry.ca   godwit@fitzhenry.ca

10 9 8 7 6 5 4 3 2 1

Library and Archives Canada Cataloguing in Publication

Beck, Carolyn, author
That squeak / Carolyn Beck ; illustrations by François Thisdale.

Issued in print and electronic formats.
ISBN 978-1-55455-293-1 (bound).–ISBN 978-1-55455-827-8 (pdf)

I. Thisdale, François, 1964-, illustrator II. Title.

PS8553.E2949T43 2015   jC813'.6   C2014-907187-6
                                                 C2014-907188-4

Publisher Cataloging-in-Publication Data (U.S)

Beck, Carolyn.
That squeak / Carolyn Beck ; illustrated by François Thisdale.
[   ] pages : color illustrations ; cm.
Also published in electronic format.
Summary: In the aftermath of the death of his best friend, Jay, Joe decides to take Jay's bike and fix it up. Carlos, the new kid in town, offers to help, but when intentions are misinterpreted, Joe realizes Jay's bike is not the only thing that needs a little care.
ISBN: 978-1-55455-293-1
ISBN: 978-1-55455-827-8 (PDF, Follet and Overdrive)
1. Friendship – Juvenile fiction. 2. Grief in children – Juvenile fiction. I. Thisdale, Francois. II. Title.
[E] dc23 PZ7.B434Th 2015

Fitzhenry & Whiteside acknowledges with thanks the Canada Council for the Arts, and the Ontario Arts Council for their support of our publishing program. We acknowledge the financial support of the Government of Canada through the Canada Book Fund (CBF) for our publishing activities.

Cover and interior design by Kong Njo
Cover image by François Thisdale

Printed in China by Sheck Wah Tong Printing Press Ltd.

To Sandra, Dog River
and those summer days so long ago.

– C.B.

To the summer of 1985 and
all the roads on which we cycled.

– F.T.

You're too young, they said.

So we sneaked.

You were on your blue Monster Man plastered with stickers. I was on my Red Devil. We pedaled fast down the grey ribbon of road that runs out the back end of town.

"Cow country!" we yelled as we passed the falling-down barn. Just around the next bend the first cows were bunched against the fence.

We stopped so close they mooed at us. Their spots were like continents, their nostrils like holes into the next universe. They stood there chewing and watching. We watched back. Once in a while a tail lifted and a great big poo gushed out. We laughed so hard we nearly let go of our bikes.

Moo.

On we rode, deep into the growing lands where the fields run yellow and green away forever. Just you and me, the cows, the crows, the cicadas, and that little squeak inside your seat.

Where the road crosses the creek, we dipped down into the cool of the woods and followed the water till it got real low and lazy. Our place.

You skipped stones. I watched.

"Joe," you said as you pulled your arm back, stone still dripping, that big shiny smile all over your face. "Like this." *Flick.*

Skip, skip, skip all the way to the other side, sometimes back a bit.

"Uh huh," I said from the big mossy boulder. I can't skip stones. No matter how hard I try, two's my limit. I watched you instead. I loved the velvety feel of the moss. I loved the smell of the water. I loved the way you closed your eyes just before you let go. I loved everything about our place.

Later you sat with me. We bit into hard green apples and watched the water spit and burp its way around the jumble of rocks. *Crunch*. I loved the way the juice bubbled up on your teeth—sort of like the river.

"Joe," you said.

"Jay," I said.

"Gotta find that squeak."

"Yeah," I said.

Just you and me and our dreams and our bikes, on most days last summer when it didn't rain.

But sometimes even then.

It's bike weather again, barely. My bike's chained here to the rack, ready to take me home from school. So's yours, except it's been waiting all winter.

Us kids park and lock on either side of it every day. No one says a word. Some don't know. The rest of us just don't say out loud: "That was Jay's bike. They forgot to come and get it."

Nobody goes to your house and knocks on your blue door and says to your parents, "I thought you should know Jay's bike's still down at the school. Been there all winter, reminding us that he's never coming back." We don't say those words. They're too hard.

We just pretend it isn't here.

I couldn't believe it, even at the funeral. Nobody believed it. *Too young*, they kept saying. *Impossible*.

But your bike's still here.

And you aren't.

It's real late. All the other kids have grabbed their bikes and scooted home. Clouds are bunching dark and low.

I should just take my bike and try to beat the rain. But instead I reach for the handlebar of your bike. Dull metal like the sky. Not like you. You were shiny.

I press my hand against the seat. There's that squeak.

We spent hours with the oil can and the wrench. We tightened and loosened, squeezed and greased. Nothing *ever* worked.

"Forget it," you said with your big shiny smile. "Let's just call it 'my squeak'."

A minute later you were complaining again. I think you liked to.

"That squeak!" you said, as you ran the chain through the rack and snapped the lock shut. October 4th. Last fall. So long ago.

The lock was the last thing on this bike you touched. By lunchtime that day…

I know the combination. Nobody will stop me.

Nobody else will touch it. *Bad luck.*

My fingers spin the dial three times around to the number sixteen, then left past forty-eight, but it keeps sticking. I have to start over again. Then again. I feel the wind sharpening up against the back of my neck. I feel tears coming. I have to take this bike home and make it shiny again.

"Whatcha doin'?"

I look up into Carlos's thin face. His long black hair is blowing back like a scarf in the wind. He came into our classroom a week ago. He looks like he never had a bike that wasn't stolen from somebody else. They say he lives in a car with his father and brother out by the old rail lines. They say they've had horrible bad luck. They say.

"I'm...uh..." *Can't he see?* "I'm taking this bike."

"Not yours?" His eyes are bright. Even on this nasty April day, I can see the shine in them, but what I notice most is how wrinkled his shirt is under that too-small sweater.

"Nope."

"Stealing it?" He laughs. His teeth are clean and white, like movie-star teeth. How do you keep clean when you live in a car?

"Why do *you* have to steal a bike?"

The lock's jammed up real good now.

"And why…" The wind whips at his voice. My fingers can't budge the lock. "Why *this* one?"

"Because I want to, okay?" I mean to snap at him, but the words come out so low he probably doesn't hear.

I blink. Blink. Blink. All I want is to take your bike home.

I fiddle with the lock like I am working hard at it when all I'm doing is working hard at not crying. Tears are getting ready to spill down my cheeks. I'm going to have to sniff in a sec and then he'll know.

Go away.

Carlos puts his hand on my shoulder. I see the moons of dirt under his fingernails. "Let me try," he says.

Spin. Spin. Spin. Sixteen. Spin. Spin. Forty-eight. Spin. Seventeen. CLICK.

Just like that, the lock is open and that place inside my chest where my feelings are twists up so tight I think it's going to bust.

"It's okay," he says. "It doesn't look like the guy's coming back for his bike."

Everything explodes at once. I hear the sound of your name bounce off the brick wall of the school. Inside my ribs, big aching sobs suck and heave like tidal waves. There's snot everywhere. And so many tears that I can't see anymore.

All the while, Carlos is there, his hand on my shoulder. He keeps saying it's all right and he's sorry for whatever he said. His voice is low and hollow and full of soft echoes.

The rain starts. It's mean and nailing, full of the last edges of winter.

Me, Carlos, and your bike in the rain.

I cry. I cry. I cry, cry, cry, cry, cry, cry, cry.

I cry till there are only empty gulps coming out and the cold and wet hurt more than my feelings do.

Carlos must be colder than I am with just that sweater on.

"I'll help you polish it up, if you like."

"No," I say. "I'll be fine."

"I know how."

"No," I say. "I'll be fine."

I don't take your bike home. I don't ride mine. I just walk and let the rain get in my eyes.

After school the next day, I wheel your bike home. Carlos wheels mine. He's carrying a bag full of rags and grease. I tell him where to put my bike in the garage, then he says, "I'll help you start."

He shows me how to rub hard and fast. We work together, me at the handlebars, him at the back. Just me and him in a sunny spot on the driveway. He's explaining what to do next, then what after that, to make the bike "shiny-like-new," he calls it.

Why? I start to ask myself. He's poor, but he's brought his own rags and grease. Why? The question makes circles in my head the way my rag makes circles on the spotty chrome.

Then I know.

He wants the bike.

All those echoes I thought I heard yesterday, his hand on my shoulder—phony. Just plotting to get your bike. I see his eyes following his own cloth along a spoke. Loving it.

"That's enough," I say gruffly.

His rag stops. "I don't mind," he says. "If you have something to do, go ahead. I like doing this. I'll put the bike back in the garage next to yours." My bike.

"No," I say.

He knows what I mean.

I watch him pack up his rags and his grease into the wrinkled paper bag.

What a liar he is. Pretending to be nice when all he wants is to get his hands on your bike. Never, not *ever*.

At the end of the driveway, he turns to wave goodbye.

"If one of these bikes gets stolen," I say loud enough for Mr. Duffy across the street to look up from his garden, "I'll know who did it."

Carlos turns away, face down, shoulders hunched into his little drab-brown sweater.

Caught at his sneaky conniving.

I follow my plan and polish your bike up as shiny as I can. I paint carefully around each sticker, the exact same blue. Under the right handlebar I put your name in red, just the way you'd sign it with a capital J and a loopy Y. Then I wheel your bike to the gas station to fill up the tires.

Who is there?

Carlos. He's cleaning windshields, hardly reaching the top parts. When he glances my way, I pretend I don't see him.

I watch him smile his phony movie-star smile when a lady gives him a tip. What a con artist.

Then I push your bike home.

A little while later, Carlos is at my door. His shirt and pants are all dirty from leaning on cars.

"Joe," he says. "What you said is not right. I do not steal bikes." I know— he *cons* people out of their bikes. He tried to do it to me.

"I helped you because you needed a friend and…" he swallows hard, "I needed one, too. Not because I wanted a bike."

I still don't believe him. I know what I know.

"I just thought you should know that." Carlos looks at his feet, but they do not move.

I know what he's waiting for. But I'm not going to say it. I wish I could slam the door in his face.

"Gotta go," I lie, pushing at the door.

Carlos sticks his sneaker in the doorway.

"Even if you offered me that bike, I couldn't take it," he says quickly. "Dad won't let me ride a bike anymore. He's afraid I'll get killed." His eyes shine brighter than ever.

"Get killed?" My hand tightens on the door knob, ready.

"Like my mom did. She was on her bike when she got run over by a truck. And she was the best cyclist in the universe. She had medals."

"You saw...?" My hand falls from the knob. My lunch is going to splat all over my shoes.

"No." Carlos glances at his feet again, takes a big, shuddery breath, then looks straight into my eyes. Straight. "But my dad did. And now he'll never let me have a bike. He'd just throw it away and yell at me for a week. So you don't have to worry. I'll never steal your bike. And that's all I wanted to say."

As he turns to go, he wipes his face on his sleeve. I feel very, very bad about what I said to him, and about his mom and all.

But somehow I feel glad, too.

"How 'bout if you sneak?" I ask him.

"Sneak?"

It's just me and Carlos and the bikes and the grey ribbon road. He's not saying anything, just smiling. He rides like the wind.

The fields are brown now, mostly really stinky mud. The cows bunched together by the fence watch us whiz by. We're going too fast to stop.

We don't slow down when we turn into the woods either. We fly over the roots and rocks. I'm glad when Carlos finally hops off, leans the bike against a stump, and runs to the water. Not our place, but that place farther down where the dead tree makes a good bench.

We sit on it, feet dangling, a gnarly knot between us like a pig's snout. The water churns by, dipping and splashing at our sneakers. It's so loud we have to shout.

I pull my pack of gum from my pocket and push a stick at him.

"Thanks, Joe," he says. I know he doesn't just mean the gum.

"We can do this any time you want," I say back.

"Until I go," he says. "Dad's talking about moving after school finishes."

"Until you go," I say, wishing he hadn't said that, not yet, anyway.

"Then we'll just be remembering," he says.

Carlos turns over onto his stomach, pulls up a sleeve, and reaches into the water. He brings up a pebble, speckled black and white, smooth and flat. He passes it to me.

"It's a skipper," I say, turning it over and over in my hand, wet and cold.

"I can't make a stone skip," he says, scrambling back to sit. "Not for anything."

"Me, neither," I say. "But I used to know someone who could skip them like water bugs. All the way to the other side and sometimes back a bit." I stop my hand, remembering.

For a long time we chew our gum and watch the water roar by.

"Tell me about Jay."

"What?" I can't believe he just said that.

He nods toward your bike leaning against the stump. Under the handlebar, plain as a cardinal in a clear sky, is the secret "Jay".

Carlos waits, his dark shiny eyes watching my face.

"Jay was my best friend." My throat flutters. "He got killed."

Carlos's hand is on my shoulder just like in the school yard. This time I'm not looking at his fingernails. I am looking straight at him and he is looking back.

"So," he says, "I'm riding a dead guy's bike."

My throat's too tight to answer.

Carlos leans to one side as he pushes his hand into his pocket. Out comes an old-fashioned change purse, striped blue and green with a clasp. He opens it carefully. His fingers pull out a shiny gold earring. It dangles in the breeze of the water.

"This is what I kept."

"I wasn't sure if I believed you," I say and as soon as I do, I know how much it must hurt him. But it is true.

"I know," he says back. "Some things are impossible."

As we follow the grey ribbon home, I watch Carlos do what he was born to do. The wind pulls his hair straight back from his face. He's squinting hard.

I can feel the tug of my own hair and the pull, like a sinker, of the stone in my pocket. I can hear the tires on the asphalt and that squeak in the seat beside me.

"Hey, Joe," Carlos yells.

"Yeah, Car?" I yell back.

"That squeak. I can fix it."

I turn my face away, to the rows of churned-up dirt in the field. "I know," I say. "But…"

There's just the tires now. And the wind. And that squeak.
   "I know." Carlos's voice comes out shrill. "You want to keep it."

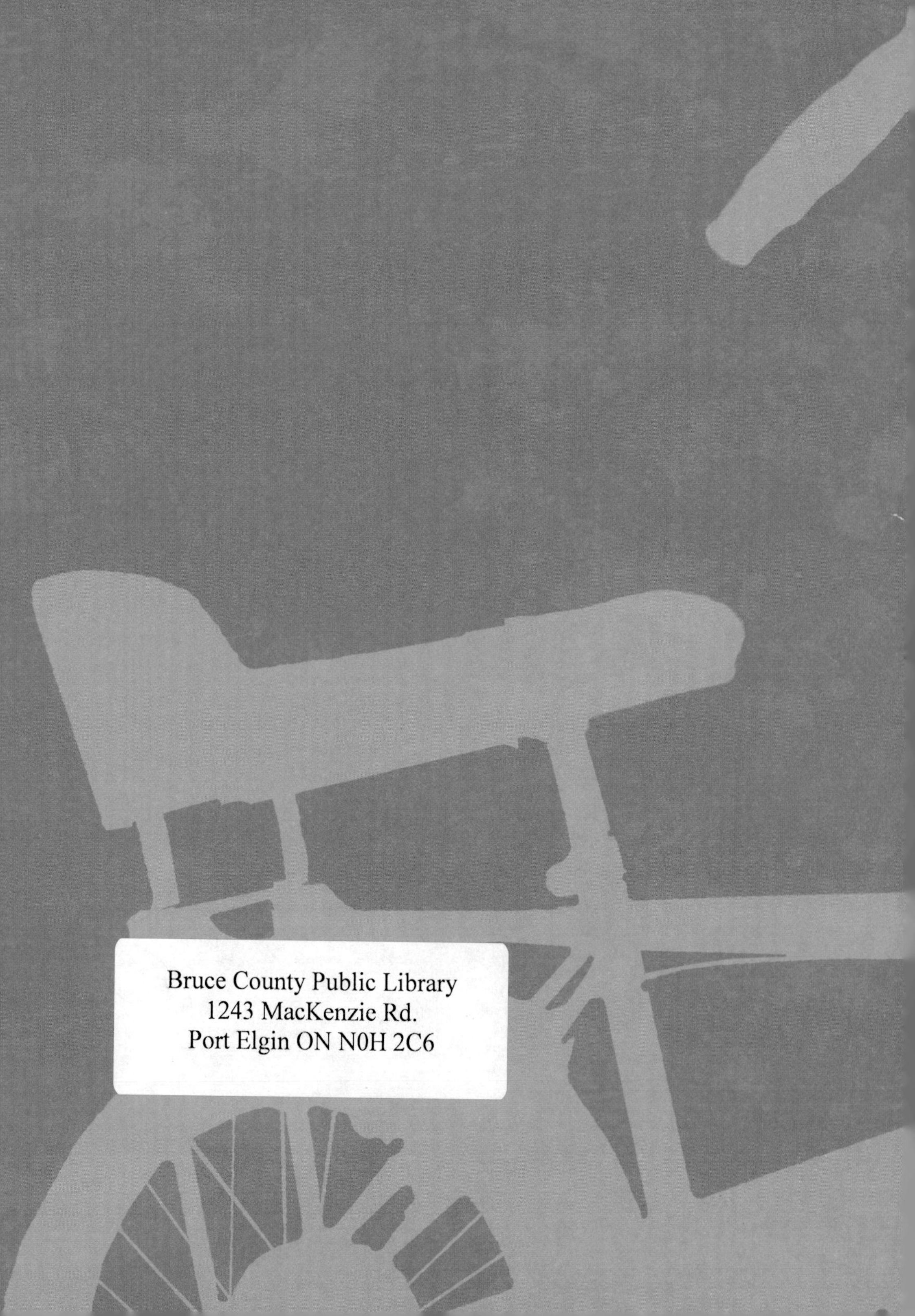